Adam and Eve's son Cain attacked his brother Abel.
You can find out what happened to the two brothers in Genesis 4:1–16.
Which boy here is Abel? Can you find all the deliberate mistakes in this picture?

Cain attacked his brother Abel.
Find ten differences between these two pictures of the brothers.
Read what happened to both of them in Genesis 4:1–16.

Abraham and Sarah were very old and they had no children.
Sarah laughed when messengers from God told Abraham she would have a son.
Find fifteen dishes in this picture. *Look up the story of Abraham's visitors in Genesis 18:1–15.*

Isaac had a half-brother named Ishmael. Ishmael was making fun of baby Isaac.
How many differences can you discover between these two pictures?
Read this story in Genesis 21:1–21. What happened to Ishmael?

After Abraham's son Isaac was born, God tested Abraham. God told him to sacrifice Isaac.
Find all the deliberate mistakes in this picture.
Did Abraham actually kill Isaac? *You can read this story in Genesis 22:1–19.*

God said to Abraham, "Don't hurt your son Isaac!"
Find ten differences between the two pictures.
You can read this story in Genesis 22:1–19. What animal did God provide as a sacrifice?

Jacob was Abraham's grandson.
Join up the dots. What is Jacob giving to his spoilt son Joseph?
You can find this story in Genesis 37:1–4.

Jacob had a big family, but loved his son Joseph more than all his other boys.
What is Joseph wearing here? Circle at least ten differences between these two pictures.
Read this story in Genesis 37:3–4.

In this picture of Joseph and his coat, the artist has made lots of deliberate mistakes.
Can you find at least seven?
Read Genesis 37:1–4. Who was Joseph's mother?

Joseph is wearing his special coat.
Can you find twelve black-headed sheep in this picture?
You can read the story of Joseph and his coat in Genesis 37:1–4.

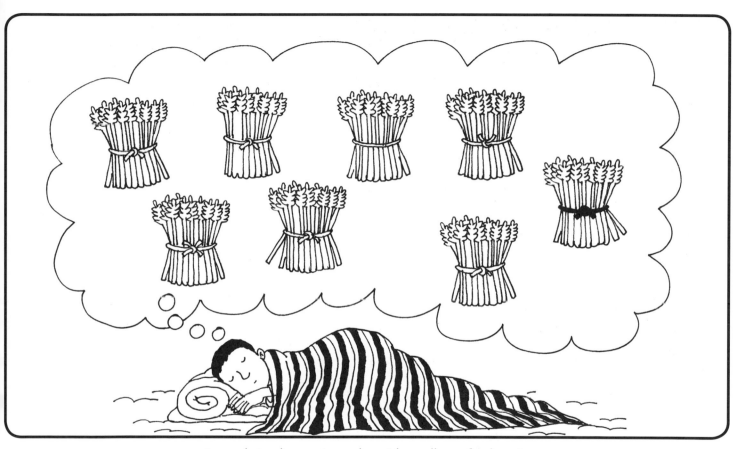

Joseph is dreaming about bundles of wheat.
Which two bundles are exactly the same? *Read Genesis 37:3–8.*
Why were his brothers so cross when Joseph told them his dream?

Baby Moses' mother hid him by the River Nile.
Join up the dots to find out where Moses' mother put him.
You can read the story of baby Moses in Exodus 2:1–10.

Baby Moses is hidden among the reeds. Why was Moses put in the water?
How many deliberate mistakes can you find here? Circle them all.
This story is in Exodus 2:1–10.

13

Here are the reeds and the ducks – but the artist has missed out Moses and his basket.
Draw them and then finish the picture with your crayons or felt-tips.
You can read this well-known story in Exodus 2:1–7.

Moses was put in a basket and hidden among the reeds of the River Nile.
Which path must the Egyptian princess take to reach baby Moses?
You can read this story in Exodus 2:1–10.

The princess of Egypt saw Moses' basket hidden among the reeds.
What is the princess saying here? Fill in her speech bubble.
Read Exodus 2:5–6 to help you.

Moses grew up as a royal prince in Egypt.
How many frogs can you find hidden here?
Read Exodus 2:7–10. What was the meaning of his name?

Can you find ten differences between these two pictures
of Moses with the princess of Egypt?
Read Exodus 2:5–6. Where did the princess first see Moses?

After she prayed to God, Hannah had a baby. She named him Samuel.
She gave her son to help in the temple. Circle all the coats hidden in this picture.
Read about Hannah's promise in 1 Samuel 1:21 – 2:11.

Hannah gave her son Samuel to help the priests in the temple.
The artist has made some mistakes. Can you find them all? Which is the funniest?
This story is in 1 Samuel 1:21 – 2:11.

Samuel's mother took him to help Eli the priest, as she had promised.
Find ten differences here between the two drawings.
You can read this story in 1 Samuel chapter 1.

Samuel now lived in the temple. All these pictures of Samuel in bed look the same.
But look carefully, and you will discover one is slightly different. Which one?
Read this story in 1 Samuel 3:1–21. Why does Samuel look surprised?

Samuel heard God call him in the night. But he thought it was the high priest, Eli!
Can you find nine crescent moons hidden in this picture?
Look up the story in 1 Samuel 3:1–21.

23

Where was Samuel when he heard God's voice calling him?
Join up the dots to find out.
You can find this story in 1 Samuel 3:1–21.

Samuel heard God calling his name one night.
Fill in the speech bubble with Samuel's answer.
Read this story in 1 Samuel 3:1–10.

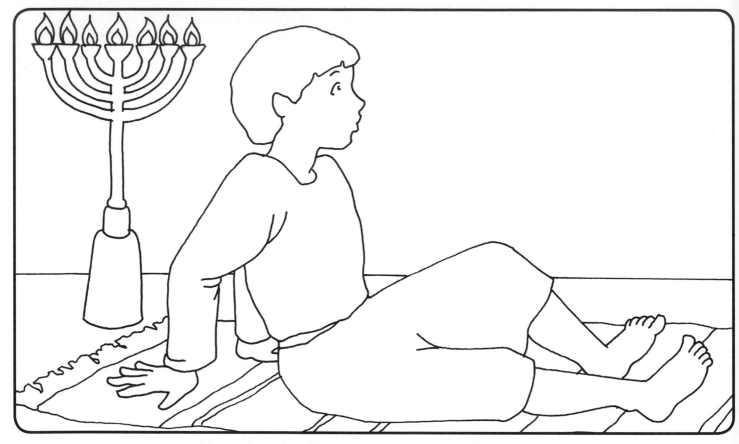

Samuel heard God calling him when he was in bed one night.
Finish this picture of Samuel listening to God with your crayons or felt-tips.
Read this story in 1 Samuel 3:1–10.

Samuel grew up to become a leader of his people.
He went to the shepherd boy David's house to anoint him as king of Israel.
Can you find eight different horns in this picture? *Look up the story in 1 Samuel 16:1–13.*

Samuel is pouring oil on David's head to show he will become the next king of Israel.
How many crazy mistakes can you find in the picture?
Read this story in 1 Samuel chapter 16.

Saul was king of Israel before David. He was often sad.
But when David played his harp, King Saul felt happier.
How many differences can you spot between these two pictures? *Read 1 Samuel 16:21–23.*

29

David loved to play the harp. How can David reach his harp?
He can walk only where the floor tiles touch.
Read the story of Saul's sadness in 1 Samuel 16:14–23.

30

David's father is giving him food to take to his brothers. They are fighting in King Saul's army.
Can you find all the apples hidden in the picture?
Read 1 Samuel 17:17–21. How many apples did you find?

David said he would fight the giant, Goliath. So King Saul offered to lend David his arms.
Find six helmets hidden in this picture. Did David use the king's arms?
Read about David and Goliath in 1 Samuel 17:38–51.

David collected five stones from the stream. He needed them to fight Goliath with his sling.
Which line must he follow to find exactly five stones?
Read 1 Samuel 17:50.

David collected five stones and put them in his bag.
What is he saying here to the giant, Goliath? Write your answer in the speech bubble.
Read 1 Samuel 17:40 and 45–47 to help you.

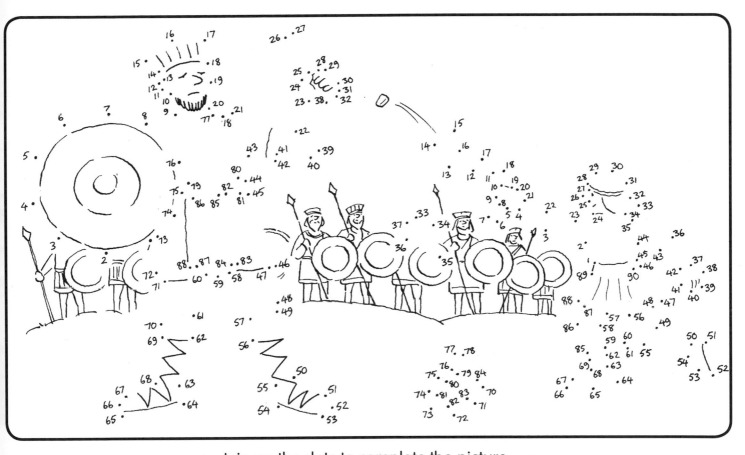

Join up the dots to complete the picture.
What did young David use to beat the terrifying giant, Goliath? (It's in his left hand.)
You can find this part of the story in 1 Samuel 17:41–51.

David is using his sling to fight the giant, Goliath.
The artist has made at least ten funny mistakes. Can you find all of them?
Read this part of the story in 1 Samuel 17:48–51.

Draw a circle around nine black stones in this picture.
Whose sword did David use to cut off Goliath's head?
Read 1 Samuel 17:51 to find out.

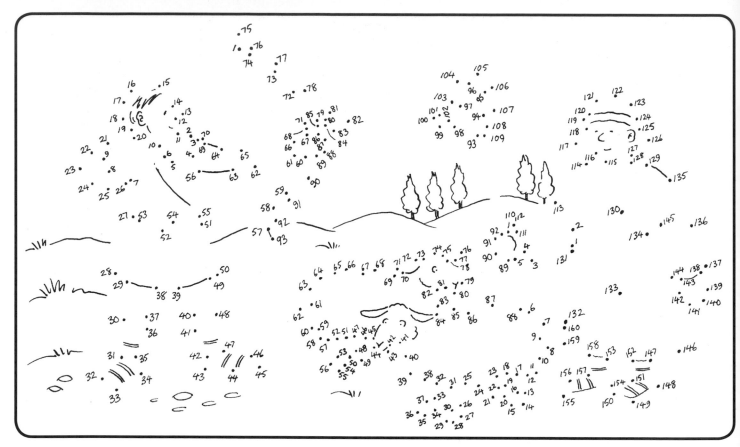

One day David and his friend Jonathan went to shoot arrows.
Join up the dots to complete this picture.
Read this story in 1 Samuel 20:18–42.

When David died, his son Solomon became king. He was very wise. People came to ask him for help. Two women argued about who a baby belonged to. They asked Solomon to decide. Join the dots to complete the picture. *Read this story in 1 Kings 3:17–27.*

Mary lived in the little village of Nazareth. The angel Gabriel came to tell her she was going to have a baby son. What was his name to be? The artist has made lots of funny mistakes. How many can you find? *You can read this story in Luke 1:26–38.*

Mary's cousin Elizabeth had a baby around the same time.
Elizabeth's husband couldn't speak, so he wrote down the baby's name. It was "John".
Can you find all the deliberate mistakes in this picture? *Read this story in Luke 1:57–66.*

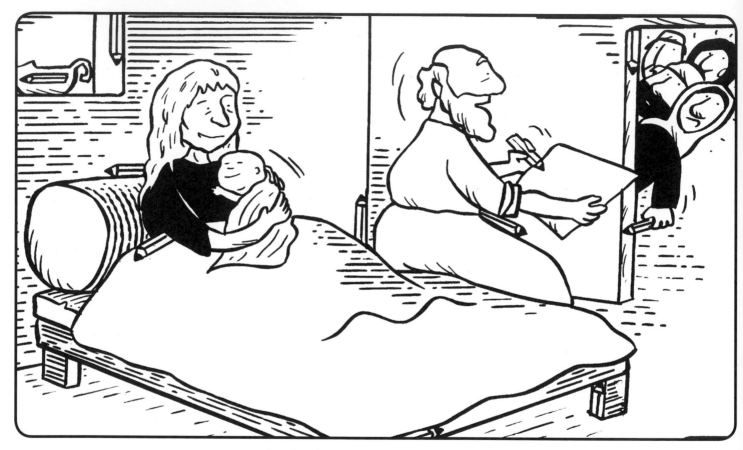

Elizabeth's son was called John.
Can you find all twelve pencils hidden in this picture?
Read the story of the birth of Elizabeth's son, John, in Luke 1:57–66.

42

Jesus was born in a stable in Bethlehem.
Join up the dots to complete the picture. What did Mary use as a cot for baby Jesus?
You can find this part of the story in Luke 2:7.

43

The wise men each brought a present for baby Jesus.
Finish this picture of the wise men, using your crayons or felt-tips.
What gifts did they bring for the baby? *Read Matthew 2:11 to find out.*

Simeon was very old when he saw baby Jesus. He was happy, because he'd been waiting for the Saviour to be born. Can you find all the artist's funny mistakes in this drawing?
Read about Simeon in Luke 2:25–35.

An angel told Joseph in a dream that it wasn't safe to stay in Bethlehem.
So Joseph took Mary and baby Jesus to Egypt.
Join up the dots to complete the picture. *Read Matthew 2:13–15.*

When it was safe again, Joseph took Mary and Jesus back home to Nazareth.
Can you find all the crazy mistakes in this picture?
Read how Jesus' family returned to Nazareth in Matthew 2:19–23.

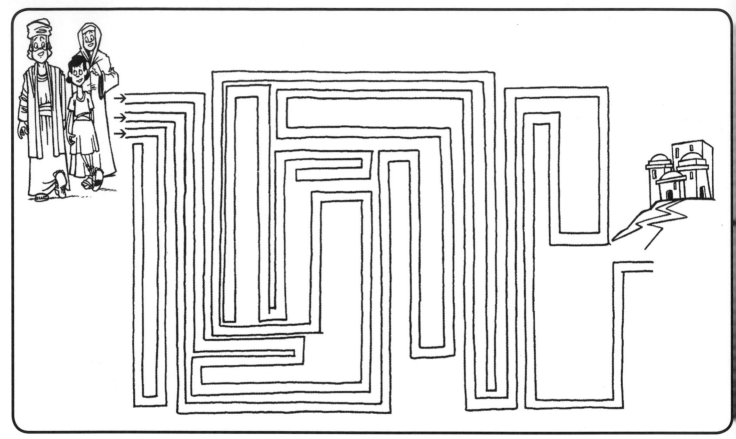

When he was twelve, Jesus went to Jerusalem with Mary and Joseph for the great festival.
Can you find the right way through the maze to the city of Jerusalem?
Read this story in Luke 2:41–52.

Jesus spent a lot of time talking to the priests in the temple.
In Jesus' time, people often wrote on scrolls wound around wooden handles.
Can you find all the scrolls hidden here? *Read this story in Luke 2:41–47.*

Jesus spent hours in the temple talking to the priests. Mary and Joseph didn't know where he was. Can you find ten differences between these two pictures?

Read this story in Luke 2:41–49. What did the priests think of Jesus?

50

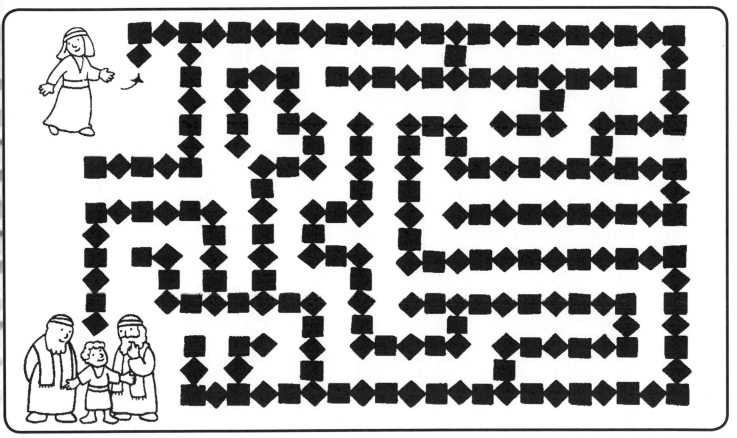

Mary is trying to find Jesus.
Help her to follow the tiles on the temple floor to find her son.
You can read about this in Luke 2:41–52.

At Jairus's house, everyone was crying because his little girl had died.
What has happened here? What is Jesus saying to Jairus's daughter?
Read the story about this little girl in Luke 8:41–42, 49–56. Now fill in Jesus' speech bubble.

Jesus brought back to life the little girl who had died. How old was she?
The artist has made lots of funny mistakes. Can you find ten?
You can read this story in your Bible. Read Mark 5:22–24, 35–43.

Jairus's daughter is alive again. Her mother is bringing her something to eat.
Complete the drawing and then fill it in with your crayons.
Read about this in Luke 8:54–56.

Jesus was talking to a huge crowd of people. Join up all the dots.
This boy gave _ _ _ fish and _ _ _ _ barley loaves to Jesus to help feed 5,000 people!
You can find this story in John 6:1–13.

This little boy gave Jesus his lunch – five barley loaves and two fish.
Which line will bring the boy to Jesus?
Read this story in John 6:1–13.

This boy has five small loaves and two little fish.
How many tiny fish can you find hidden in this picture?
Read this story in John 6:1–13. What did Jesus do with the boy's food?

Here are six pictures of Jesus and the boy with loaves and fishes.
Which two pictures are exactly the same?
Read this story in John 6:1–13.

Once Jesus fed a crowd of more than 5,000 people.
Which disciple brought the boy's bread and fish to Jesus?
Can you find ten crazy mistakes made by the artist? *You can read about this in John 6:1–13.*

Jesus told a story about a boy who left his home and his family.
Help the boy to return to his loving father.
You can read about this in Luke 15:11–32.

Here is the father waiting to greet his lost son.
Complete the picture by drawing the boy coming home.
Read Luke 15:17–27. What did the father tell his servants to do?

Here are six pictures from the story of the boy who left home – but they've all been mixed up.
Number them in the right order.
Read the whole story in Luke 15:11–32 to help you.

Jesus told a story about ten bridesmaids.
These bridesmaids are waiting for the groom. Each is holding a lamp.
Which girl is the odd one out? *Read this story in Matthew 25:1–13.*

These bridesmaids are all waiting for the bridegroom to arrive.
Find ten differences between the two pictures.
Read Jesus' story about the bridesmaids in Matthew 25:1–13.